Hands On The World Environmental Series

Johnny & The Old Oak Tree

A Message About
Paper Recycling

Story by Rachael Peterpaul Paulson
Illustrated by Delton Gerdes

Hands On The World Books
Crestmont Publishing
Houston, Texas

Crestmont Publishing
P.O. Box 57176
Webster, TX 77598

Publisher's Cataloging in Publication
Paulson, Rachael Peterpaul.
  Johnny & the old oak tree / Story by Rachael Peterpaul Paulson;
  illustrated by Delton Gerdes.
  p. cm.–(Hands on the world environmental series)
  ISBN 0-9642296-0-9
  L C C N 94-68608

  1. Environmentalism–Juvenile fiction. 2. Recycling (Waste, etc.)–Juvenile
fiction. 3. Recycling (Waste)–Fiction. I. Gerdes, Delton, ill. II. Title. III. Title:
Johnny and the old oak tree.

PZ7.P3857Joh 1995   [Fic]
QBI94-177

*In memory of my little brother Johnny, my guardian angel,
who has guided me throughout this book.*

From the heavens, may you help protect the earth.

To Dad. Thanks for the gift of storytelling.

R.P.

Many thanks to:

Mom and Dad, for their loving support.

Mike, my husband, for driving the whole family, dog included,
from Texas to Connecticut to present my manuscript.

My two children, Danielle and Mikey, for inspiring me, posing for
pictures and for putting up with those peanut butter sandwich dinners.

The extended Peterpaul family in New Jersey, for their interest,
excitement and help on the manuscript.

To all the Paulsons, who took the time to edit and read.

Martha, for those long, happy hours of practical advice on the manuscript.

Russell White, for leading me. Kern, for being an angel.

Carolyn Merritt, for believing in me.

Author Joe Vitale, mentor, for guiding me.

My many friends, Larry, Lisa, Lori, Pat, Jackie, Cheryl, Terri, Maria,
Debbie and all of those on Capehill for their endless support.

Sally and those at Jeremy's Bookshelf for answering my many questions.

Kevin Lewis, for helpful suggestions.

Artist Delton Gerdes, for sharing his gift with me.

All the children and teachers who took part in the manuscript,
especially those at L.L. Pugh Elementary.

Pete, for putting it all together.

John H., for making my dream come true.

Dear Parents and Teachers,

Three years ago, my two-year-old daughter Danielle asked me about the stack of newspapers in the corner of the kitchen. When I tried to explain recycling to her, she was full of questions. As her curiosity grew, so did my determination to give her answers, and I decided to develop a story to help her understand.

I quickly realized how little I really knew and embarked on a fact finding mission that led me in many directions. I was encouraged to learn that many of us are making an effort to educate our children about caring for our world, but also concerned to discover that most of our children are missing out on a great deal of accurate information.

When visiting schools, I made sure to ask the students the one question that was always guaranteed to elicit an active response. Why do we recycle? Although a wide range of answers would come forth, I was very surprised to find that "because we have too much trash" was rarely mentioned as an important reason to recycle. Many children did not know where their trash actually went once it left their homes, and the word "landfill" was virtually unknown to most of them. However, once the students were given information about recycling and our landfill problem, they always had a wealth of ideas about how they could make a difference – many of which formed the basis of my book.

Throughout my research I've been fortunate to witness first hand how motivated children can become once they begin to understand the impact they can have on the environment. I can only hope that my story will broaden their knowledge, increase their enthusiasm, and motivate them to make a difference.

Maybe then they will know H.O.W. to help change the world!

Rachael Peterpaul Paulson

Rachael Peterpaul Paulson
Hands On the World Books

There once was a boy named Johnny.
His best friend in the whole world was a
tree – that's right, a tree!

Nestled in the branches of this great
oak was the most magnificent treehouse
you have ever seen. When Johnny was a
baby, his dad built this treehouse just for
him. Johnny was always playing and
crawling under the spreading shade of
the old oak. As soon as he could
walk, he was climbing the steps
that became a part of the old
tree's huge, gray trunk.

Protected by the tree's gigantic umbrella, each landing of his treehouse carried Johnny on a new adventure. He talked to the oak and made the tree a part of his imaginary world. His leafy friend was always there for him. Together, they traveled into the land of make believe. Johnny was happy to have his tree. He only wished the old oak would talk back to him.

One Spring day while Johnny was pretending to guard the castle in his tree house, his wish came true.

He had eaten most of his peanut butter sandwich and now watched through his cardboard binoculars as the birds and squirrels ate the bread crust he had scattered.

Suddenly, the wind began to blow. The brown paper bag that his lunch had been packed in went flying to the ground. The tree began to sway and shake, and the oak's branches started to pound against the sides of his castle as if they were trying to get his attention. He thought he heard a voice – or was it just the wind?

Johnny put his sword in his back pocket and climbed up to his space station landing. Bare feet spread, he stood there, frozen in place, moving only his eyes as he searched around him. All was still.

Then he heard the sound again. It *was* a voice! Someone was calling his name. It was flowing in the breeze.

"J...o...h...n...n...y." He looked up into the tree's branches, and squinting, he asked, "Tree, are you calling me?"

A deep but gentle voice said, "Yes, my friend. I need to talk to you about our earth."

Johnny stood very still. His heart skipped a beat and his eyes grew large. "My wish has come true!" he shouted. He wrapped his arms around the tree's huge trunk. He was filled with happiness.

"Come," said the tree. "Climb up here where I can hold you."

Quickly, Johnny climbed up into the tree's branches and rested his head in a pillow of leaves. The old oak slowly rocked the boy and said, "Our earth is sad, Johnny, and needs your help. The land is disappearing under mountains of trash called *landfills*." Johnny could feel the softness of the tree's leaves brushing against his face. He listened very carefully as the tree continued.

"People are throwing away too many things my friend," said the old oak. "The earth's land is being used to hold all of this trash."

Johnny lifted his head and sat up. "But I thought the garbage truck ate all of our trash," he said.

The wise old tree snuggled him closely and said, "That would be wonderful, Johnny, but the garbage truck carries your trash to a hole in the land where it is dumped."

"You mean the land gets filled up with trash? Is that why it is called a landfill?" Johnny asked.

"That's right," said the tree. "You see, Johnny, all of this trash is covered with dirt. The sun, air, and even the insects and animals try to break the trash apart, but they can no longer reach it after it is buried so deeply." "So what happens to it?" Johnny asked. "Sometimes, it stays there for years," said the old oak. "Trash is taking over our land, Johnny. Our earth must be protected!"

Johnny sat up and cried out, "I'll protect the earth! If that trash tries to take over our land, I'll take this sword and I'll...I'll..."

"No, Johnny!" the tree interrupted. "That will not solve our problem. Our earth wants you to know that *recycling* can help to save our land."

Johnny stuck his sword in his pocket and asked, "What's recycling?"

The tree's branches brushed against the binoculars that rested upon Johnny's chest.

"This is recycling," said the old oak. Johnny grinned. "I made these binoculars in school," he said, holding them in his hands. "Yes," said the old oak, "you took used cardboard rolls and made something new."

"That is how you recycle, my friend. You see, Johnny, if you use things over again, there is less trash," said the old oak. The tree's branches moved from side to side.

"Look around you, Johnny," said the old oak. "Plants, animals, and insects don't leave any trash in their world. Why do you think that is so?"

Johnny looked through his binoculars as nature's magical kingdom grew large. He watched as his bread crust disappeared. He saw the oak's fallen leaves being carried underground by the ants. Those leaves would soon become a part of the soil. He could not believe his eyes. "WOW!" Johnny said. "They're using our leftovers. That's why they don't leave any trash." He laughed when he noticed his old shoe lace was a part of the blue jay's nest. "They don't waste anything," Johnny said.

"That's right!" said the old oak. "Nature recycles things all the time."

Johnny reached for a branch and hung there for awhile.

Dropping back onto his treehouse landing he asked, "Can you tell me more about recycling?"

The tree's leaves danced in the sunlight when Johnny asked this question. Its branches moved in time with each spoken word.

"Oh Johnny, recycling can change the world," said the oak excitedly. "If each person on this earth used things over again, there would be fewer landfills. The earth's land would be cleaner and much more beautiful."

Johnny closed his eyes for a moment. A spring breeze brought movement to the treehouse. He imagined his landing to be a magic carpet, flying him over a perfectly clean world.

Below him, tree tops sparkled. He saw rolling, green hills covered with flowers that reached for the clean, blue sky. Moving from side to side, he pretended to dodge the mountain tops covered with puffy, white snow.

He zoomed down closer where he could see the clear, blue water.
It looked like a sheet of ice glittering in the sunshine.

He could see all the way to the water's bottom. Looking around him, he saw so much color and life.

Amazed, Johnny opened his eyes and said, "I wish I could make the whole world look that clean and beautiful."

"You can my friend," said the old oak. "You see, Johnny, our earth is in your hands. You can help to change the world."

"But I'm not a grown-up," Johnny said. "What can I do?"

"You can start by thinking before you throw things in the trash can," said the old oak.

At that moment, a blue jay squawked as it flew from its nest onto the edge of a trash can in the backyard. Johnny turned his head to look. He noticed that the trash can was stacked with newspapers.

"Will all of that paper go to a landfill?" Johnny asked.

"Yes," said the old oak. "A lot of paper is thrown away."

Johnny thought he heard a sadness in the tree's voice.

He lowered his eyes. Softly he said, "I know that paper is made from trees. Are you sad that my family is using so much paper?" he asked.

"No Johnny," said the old oak. "It's only the *waste* of paper that makes me so unhappy. Sometimes people throw away perfectly good paper."

The tree and Johnny were quiet for a moment.

The old oak spoke again. "If you could think of ways to use paper over again, Johnny, you could make a big difference."

Johnny thought long and hard. The words "USE AGAIN" started humming through his mind. He thought about all the things he used in one day that were made of paper; there were so many. How could he use them over again?

Suddenly, Johnny's eyes lit up. "How about all of the paper I use at school? If I use both sides, would that help the earth?" he asked.

"Yes," said the oak happily. "Can you imagine how much paper would be saved if your whole class did that?"

"How about if my family doesn't use as many paper cups and plates – would that help?" Johnny asked.

"Oh yes," said the oak. "Reducing your use of paper would be a very good thing. That means less trash!"

Johnny could feel the tree's happiness. He knew the oak was smiling under its crusty bark.

The blue jay squawked again, bringing Johnny's attention back to the paper stacked in the trash can. "But what about those newspapers?" Johnny asked in a worried voice.

The oak lightly placed a branch on the boy's shoulder and said, "There is also another way to recycle, Johnny. There are special factories that mash used paper into a paste called pulp. This pulp is used to make new paper."

Johnny pointed to the filled trash can. "You mean they can do that with those newspapers?" he asked.

"Yes, they can. If enough newspapers are collected, a truck will take them to the factory. This would keep those newspapers out of our landfills."

Johnny shouted happily, "I'll tell all my friends about this. We'll collect so many newspapers - you wait and see - they'll be stacked so high they'll touch the clouds!"

Johnny was excited and the tree's leaves twinkled like crystal.

In the distance, Johnny noticed the orange-red sun going down to rest. He looked up at the oak and said, "I have to go now." "Yes," said the old tree. "It is time to say good-bye, my friend. I am very proud of you."

Johnny pressed his cheek against the tree's rugged bark. He held the tree close to him. "You're my best friend," he said softly.

Then, silence surrounded the tree as dusk settled around them. Even the birds and crickets were quiet.

Johnny's head was full of ideas. He was ready to tell everyone what he had learned. There was so much to do. He hurried down the tree.

As he ran toward his house, Johnny noticed the brown paper bag that his peanut butter sandwich had been packed in, lying on the ground. He quickly picked it up and tossed it into an empty cardboard box that was sitting next to the trash can. "Bull's eye!" he shouted.

And then he *remembered*. That bag was clean, he thought. He turned and looked at the old oak. Quickly, he reached into the box to rescue his brown bag. Folding it neatly, he told himself that he would use the same bag for lunch tomorrow and the next day, too! Then, he took another look at the big box. "I could turn that into a great truck," he said aloud. That would help to protect the earth from trash.

As Johnny reached the back door of his house, he turned for a last look at his wonderful tree.

He stepped back in amazement as he looked at the sky. The earth had created the most beautiful rainbow he had ever seen. A big grin stretched across Johnny's face. He knew that his friend the old oak was right.

He COULD change the world!

PROJECT IDEA

St. Judes Ranch

NEEDS: your used greeting cards (fronts only).
These cards are recycled to make new greeting cards.

St. Judes Ranch for Children is a non-profit organization that
provides a home for abused and neglected children.

Send Cards to:

St. Judes Ranch for Children
100 St. Judes Street
Boulder City, NV 89005

*Make your
own paper.
See recipe
on following pages.*

Free Comic Book and Poster.
* See following pages for other publications and phone number.

RECIPE FOR
RECYCLED PAPER

WHAT TO DO:

MAKING THE FRAME
Use a can opener to remove both ends of a coffee can.
(Carefully dispense of the sharp lid pieces.)

Cut the center out of the plastic lid, leaving a thin border of plastic near the outside rim.

Cut out a circle of netting just larger than the opening of the coffee can. Place the netting over one end of the coffee can and snap the lid over the netting to hold it in place.

MAKING THE PULP
Cut newspaper into squares of 1" or smaller.
Put 1 cup of paper squares and 4-5 cups of water into a blender. Stir on LOW for 30 seconds. Blend on HIGH until the pulp looks like a thin milk shake. (Instead of a blender, you can put the newspaper squares into a coffee can and let it sit overnight to soften. When softened, stir with a large spoon or eggbeater to make a thin pulp.)

MAKING THE PAPER
Hold the coffee can frame, with the netting end down, over a pan or bucket.

Pour 1/3 cup of paper pulp into the coffee can, covering the netting evenly.
(Add more pulp if needed.)

Let the water drain out.

Carefully remove the can from the lid and set aside.

*You may add dried, pressed flowers, glitter, yarn pieces or other decorations to the pulp at this time.

Put another piece of netting on top of the pulp.

Press down on the new "paper" with a sponge to soak up water and smooth out the fibers.

Let the newly made paper dry overnight. Your recycled paper can be cut into hearts or other shapes to make a card or framed to make a beautiful gift!

Experiment with different kinds of used paper (pages from phone books or magazines), and even grasses or cloth fibers. Try adding food coloring to make different colors of paper. Use your imagination to make your own creative designs!

GLOSSARY

Cardboard – A thin, stiff material made of paper pulp, and used in making cartons and other forms of packaging.

Earth – The planet on which we live, composed of oceans and land masses and surrounded by an atmosphere of gases. Also, the land surface of the world.

Garbage – Originally, spoiled or waste food that was thrown out: now, any matter considered worthless, unnecessary, or offensive, and usually thrown away.

Landfill – A specially engineered site for disposing of solid waste on land, constructed so that it will reduce hazard to public health and safety. Some quantities include an impermeable lower layer to block the movement of leachate in ground water, a leachate collection system, gravel layers permitting the control of methane, and daily covering of garbage with soil.

Leachate – Liquid that has percolated through solid waste and/or has been generated by solid waste decomposition, and that has dissolved or suspended materials in it. The liquid may contaminate ground or surface water.

Paper – A thin material made of pulp from wood, rag or other fibrous material and used for writing, printing, or wrapping.

Pulp – A mixture of fibrous material such as wood, rags and paper ground up and moistened to be used in making paper or cardboard.

Recycle – The process of collecting materials from the waste stream and separating them by type, remaking them into new products, and marketing and reusing the material as new products.

Reuse – The use of a product more than once in its same form for the same purpose. For example, a soft-drink bottle is reused when it is returned to the bottling company for refilling; a peanut butter jar may be reused in the home as a container for leftover food.

Trash – Material considered worthless, unnecessary, or offensive that is usually thrown away. Generally defined as dry waste material, excludes food waste and ashes. The term is often used interchangeably with the word garbage.

Waste – Material that has been discarded because it has worn out, is used up, or is no longer needed, such as packing, newspapers and used writing paper, and broken appliances. Many things thrown out as waste may have the potential to be recycled or reused.

ENVIRONMENTAL PROTECTION AGENCY
RECYCLING RESOURCES

The following EPA publications are available at no charge through the Agency's RCRA Hotline. Call 1-800-424-9346 Monday through Friday, 8:30 a.m. to 7:30 p.m. EST. For the hearing impaired, the number is TDD (800) 553-7571. In Washington, D.C., call (703) 920-9810 or TDD (703) 486-3323.

Recycle Today! A series of five publications aimed at educators and students:

  • Recycle Today! An Educational program for grades K-12 (EPA/530-sw-90-025). A concise pamphlet explaining the goals and objectives of EPA's educational recycling program and the four resources listed below.

  • Let's Reduce and Recycle! A Curriculum for Solid Waste Awareness (EPA/530-SW90-005). A booklet of lessons and activities to teach students in grades K-12 about solid waste generation and management. It teaches a variety of skills, including science, vocabulary, mathematics, and creative writing.

  • School Recycling Programs: A Handbook for Educators (EPA/530-Sw-90-023). A handy manual with step-by-step instructions on how to set up a school recycling program.

★ • Adventures of the Garbage Gremlin: Recycle and Combat a Life of Grime (EPA/530-SW-90-024). A comic book introducing students in grades 4-7 to the benefits of recycling.

★ • Ride the Wave of the Future: Recycle Today! (EPA/530-SW-90-010). A colorful poster designed to appeal to all grade levels that can be displayed in conjunction with recycling activities or used to help foster recycling.

Parents and teachers may also request a free copy of the Municipal Solid Waste Fact book (EPA/530-C-93-001), a computerized reference manual for use on PC's running MicroSoft Windows, available on disc in 3-1/2" or 5-1/4" format.

Watch for the
next story about
Johnny & The Old Oak Tree
and look for . . .

Rachael Peterpaul Paulson

Rachael Peterpaul Paulson grew up in the city of Roselle, New Jersey. She earned a degree in early childhood education and went on to be certified in Special Education. She has more than 10 years of teaching experience. She now lives in Texas with her husband Mike and their two children, and spends her time writing and presenting environmental workshops.

"A wonderful story that teaches children, very simply, how the earth and nature work together and how we must protect them."

–Minerva Perez
Channel 13 News / ABC Affiliate
Houston Read Commission

"Paulson's charming story brings ecology to the child's level. Teachers and parents will appreciate the excellent recycling activities. This book will be a great teaching tool."

–Carole Duncan Buckman
Librarian
St. Ignatius Martyr Grade School
Austin, Texas

"This story sends out a strong message without preaching and excites the child's mind at the same time."

–Dr. Paul Risk
T.L.L. Professor of Forestry
Director, Center for Resource Communication & Interpretation
Stephen F. Austin State University
Nacogdoches, Texas

"A great lesson . . . it made us want to shout to the world: Reduce, Reuse and Recycle! We wanted the story to go on and on."

–The Environmental Challenger Newsletter
Students of L.L. Pugh Elementary
Houston, Texas

"After experiencing the enthusiastic response in my second grade class, I am convinced that this book is able to instill the commitment to recycling which is so imperative to their future. The story inspires, motivates and is delightful reading."

–Barbara Manno
Second Grade Teacher
Roselle, New Jersey

"This book is inspirational literature: a wonderful teaching tool and an imaginative springboard into learning."

–Lori Brownell
Fourth Grade Teacher
Republic Michigamme School
Republic, Michigan

"The story is personable, tender and unique. The message is a very strong one, yet it is tempered by a spirit and humanity that is bound to catch the attention of all who engage in it. The illustrations are phenomenal!"

–Shelly Sentyrz
Environmental Educator
Praire City, Iowa

CREDITS

Cover and illustrations – Delton Gerdes

Design, layout and production – Delton Gerdes

Production assistance – Brocky Brown

Photography – James B. Robinson

Printing – Jolley Printing

Typography – Cherry Mallia

Color Separations – Color Separations, Inc.

Editing – Jackie Hutto and Becky Parks

Word Processing – Mike Paulson, Terri Szkirpan, Nikki and James Robinson

Marketing Manager – Ben McDonald, Word Services Inc.

Printed in U.S.A.
Printed on Champion International Corporation's recycled paper:
Kromekote Cover Recycled and Benefit Text Recycled

Goodnight Waco

1845
BOOKS

Goodnight Waco

Presented by The Junior League of Waco

ILLUSTRATED BY DIRK FOWLER

© 2021 by 1845 Books, an imprint of Baylor University Press
Waco, Texas 76798

Illustrations by Dirk Fowler
Written by Paige Connell, Ellen Derrick, Lindsey Stevens, and Stacie Virden
Book Design by Kasey McBeath

The Library of Congress has cataloged this book under ISBN 978-1-4813-1714-6.
Library of Congress Control Number: 2021917260

Printed by Friesens Corporation, Altona, Manitoba, Canada.

The Junior League of Waco is an organization of women committed to promoting voluntarism, developing the potential of women, and improving our community through the effective action and leadership of trained volunteers. Since 1935, the Junior League of Waco has donated millions of volunteer service hours and gifted more than $2 million in direct funding to community involvement projects. The Junior League of Waco celebrates its 85th anniversary with the publication of *Goodnight Waco*, which will be donated to pre-kindergarten students around the city.

This book is dedicated to the women and children of McLennan County and to the members of the Junior League of Waco who have volunteered tirelessly for the past 85 years to make our community a better place in which to live.

In the heart of Texas
is a beautiful town

where friends say goodnight
as the sun goes down.

Goodnight Huaco Tribe,
who made Waco their home.

Goodnight trails where
cowboys once roamed.

Goodnight downtown
and Heritage Square.

Goodnight red letters that
can be seen from everywhere.

Goodnight lions, giraffes,
and monkeys, too.

Goodnight all creatures at the
Cameron Park Zoo.

Goodnight lake and
goodnight boats.

Goodnight ducks
that swim and float.

Goodnight hospitals and
goodnight doctors.

Goodnight ambulances
and helicopters.

Goodnight rodeo and
goodnight fair.

Goodnight music
that fills the air.

Goodnight stadium with
victories so bold.

Goodnight fans in your
green and gold.

Goodnight Magnolia with
your silos so tall.

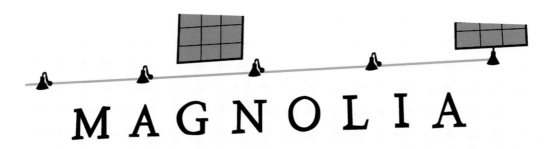

*Goodnight visitors in
groups large and small.*

Goodnight Dr Pepper and
bears that roar.

Goodnight until tomorrow at
10:00, 2:00, and 4:00.

Goodnight students,
teachers, and books.

Goodnight future nurses
and pilots and cooks.

Goodnight Texas Rangers
standing proud and tall.

Goodnight festivals and
museums for all.

Goodnight Lions Park,
train, and merry-go-round.

Goodnight Waco Mammoths
and your bones in the ground.

Goodnight Waco,
it's time to rest.

Goodnight to all whom
we love best!

Goodnight Waco

checklist

As you visit these Waco treasures,
place a checkmark by each location.

- [ ] Clifton House, headquarters of the Junior League of Waco

- [ ] Waco Suspension Bridge

- [ ] Heritage Square

- [ ] ALICO Building

- [ ] Cameron Park Zoo

- [ ] Lake Waco

- [ ] Heart O' Texas Fair & Rodeo

- [ ] McLane Stadium

- [ ] Magnolia Market at the Silos

- [ ] Baylor Bear Habitat

- [ ] Dr Pepper Museum

- [ ] Texas Ranger Hall of Fame & Museum

- [ ] Mayborn Museum

- [ ] Lions Park and Carousel

- [ ] Waco Mammoth National Monument

Thank you to these past presidents of the
JUNIOR LEAGUE OF WACO
for their generous sponsorship of *Goodnight Waco.*

Tommye Lou Davis	1982-1983	Carol Jo Mize	2007-2008
Alice Ogden	1988-1989	Susie Oliver	2008-2009
LuAnn Browder	1991-1992	Merryl Jones	2009-2010
Debbie Luce	1993-1994	Elisa Rainey	2010-2011
Jill McCall	1994-1995	Len Brown	2011-2012
Lisa Jaynes	1997-1998	Leslie Rhea	2012-2013
Cathy Pleitz	1998-1999	Erin DuBois	2013-2014
Debra Burleson	1999-2000	Laura Indergard	2014-2015
Sheryl Swanton	2000-2001	Ellen Derrick	2015-2016
Cheryl Allen	2001-2002	Beth Armstrong	2016-2017
Dianne Sawyer	2002-2003	Lanissa Willis	2017-2018
Rene Taylor	2003-2004	Holly Burchett	2018-2019
Kathy Douthit	2004-2005	Jana Hixson	2019-2021
Angela Tekell	2005-2006	Caitlyn Remson	2021-2023
Missy Larson	2006-2007		